For Nancy, with love   MK

To all the Sparkies   VL

First American edition 1993

Text copyright © 1992 by Monica Kulling
Illustrations copyright © 1992 by Vicky Lowe

Bradbury Press
Macmillan Publishing Company
866 Third Avenue
New York, NY 10022

Maxwell Macmillan Canada, Inc.
1200 Eglinton Avenue East
Suite 200
Don Mills, Ontario M3C 3N1

Macmillan Publishing Company is part of the Maxwell Communication Group of Companies.

First published in 1992 in Great Britain by All Books for Children, London.
Printed and bound in Hong Kong
10   9   8   7   6   5   4   3   2   1

Library of Congress Cataloging-in-Publication Data
Kulling, Monica.
Waiting for Amos / by Monica Kulling ; illustrated by Vicky Lowe.
— 1st American ed.
p.   cm.
Summary: Although the other animals think that he is wasting his
time, Homer the frog continues to wait for his friend to meet him as promised.
ISBN 0-02-751245-2
[1. Frogs—Fiction.   2. Animals—Fiction.   3. Friendship—
Fiction.]   I. Lowe, Vicky, ill.   II. Title.
PZ7.K9490155Wai   1993
[E]—dc20   92-19550

Waiting for Amos

Written by
Monica Kulling

Illustrated by
Vicky Lowe

Bradbury Press • New York

Maxwell Macmillan Canada • Toronto
Maxwell Macmillan International
New York • Oxford • Singapore • Sydney

Homer hopped onto the
gray-brown rock. He looked
with his frog eyes to the left.
He looked with his frog eyes
to the right.

      No Amos in sight.

"No Amos anywhere that I can see," said Homer.
"But Amos said he'd meet me this morning.
He said to wait on the gray-brown rock.
He said to wait, so wait I will."

Homer snapped a
big, juicy fly with his
long, sticky tongue.

Just then Homer's friends the Ravens flapped down beside him. They wanted to know what he was doing.

"Waiting," said Homer.

"Waiting is not *doing*," replied Jack.

"Do something," said Mabel.

"That's right," agreed Jack. "Fly or caw or rummage."

Mabel was already busy scratching the dust around the rock to see what she could find.

Homer blinked.

"Amos said to wait
on the gray-brown rock.
He said he'd be here soon,"
Homer told them, and grinned
a wide, froggy grin.

"Soon?" said Jack. "You
know how slow Amos is. Soon's
not a word he knows. Amos probably
won't even get here today. I bet you a
basket of beetles!"

"He'll be here,"
said Homer.
"Come back
at noon, and
you'll see.
And don't
forget the beetles!"

Jack and Mabel called
out, "Bye, Homer!" and
flew back to their nest.

Soon Amanda Salamander slithered into sight. "What's Homer doing?" she wanted to know.

"Waiting for Amos," said Homer.

"Waiting always makes me tired," said Amanda. "Why don't you go home to bed? It's a perfect day for sleeping. Besides, Amos is forgetful. He's probably already forgotten he's supposed to meet you here. You'll be sitting on that old rock all day for nothing."

"No, I won't," said Homer. "Amos is my friend. He knows I'm waiting for him."

Amanda called to her friend Florence Lizard. "Homer is waiting," she told Florence.

"I don't know how you can wait without getting hungry," said Florence. "You should go home and eat flies." She was watching a big, fat horsefly buzzing around the rock.

"I can eat
flies from where
I'm sitting." Homer
shot out his tongue
and swallowed.
"See?" he said.

"Homer," said Amanda, "we'll bet you a sack of cicadas that Amos doesn't show up." Florence nodded, as she settled down in the warm earth near the rock, her eyes closing.

It certainly was a perfect
day for sleeping, and Homer
did feel like going home for
just a tiny nap. But Amos
would arrive soon, and Homer didn't want to miss him.

"Go home and sleep if you like," he said. "But Amos
will be here by noon. You'll see. Instead of sleeping,
you two should get busy and collect those cicadas."

"Good-bye, Homer," said Amanda and Florence
as they slipped away.

Before long, Ogden came by.
"What's new?" he asked.
    "Nothing," replied Homer.
"I'm waiting for Amos."
    "Waiting is boring," said Ogden.
"Try something exciting.
Like swimming or hopping
or jumping."

He clambered onto the
back of the rock

and leapt as far
as he could.

"Now's not the time for doing something exciting," replied Homer. "Amos told me to wait for him. Right here. So waiting is what I'm doing."

"You'll grow old waiting for pokey Amos. I'll bet you a flask of fireflies he never gets here."

The sun rose
and the sun rose,
and soon it was
noon. Homer
was still sitting on the
gray-brown rock. All his
friends were gathered around
waiting for Amos.
But where was Amos?

Homer looked right
and Homer looked
left. But there
was no Amos.
Anywhere.

Homer was just about ready to give up
waiting when the gray-brown
rock he'd been sitting on
moved. It woke up and
popped out its head.

"Here I am, Homer!" shouted
Amos. "Right on time and plenty
hungry. I hope your friends have
brought lots to eat!" said Amos.